For Charlie and Billy with love
~ M. C. B.

For Amelia Bahrani
~ T. M.

Text copyright © M. Christina Butler 2012
Illustrations copyright © Tina Macnaughton 2012
Original edition published in English by Little Tiger Press,
an imprint of Magi Publications, London, England, 2012
LTP/1800/0295/1011 • Printed in China

Congress Cataloging-in-Publication Data available.

Mouse
and the
Moon

M. Christina Butler

Illustrated by Tina Macnaughton

Good Books

Intercourse, PA 17534, 800/762-7171
www.GoodBooks.com

Little Harvest Mouse lived by himself
in a field of grain. Every night the warm
summer breezes rocked his cozy nest, and
his friend the moon watched over him
from the deep blue sky.

Before Mouse closed his eyes each night,
he sang a lullaby to his very own moon.
　　But one evening, a cold wind rustled
through the field, and Little Harvest
Mouse couldn't see his friend anywhere.

Mouse peeked out of his nest. Everything looked
so different without the moon's friendly glow.
Trembling, he raced across the field.
"Someone's stolen the moon!" he shouted.

"Stolen the moon?" quacked Duck. "I can't believe that! The moon is in the pond where she always is."

"In the pond?" thought Mouse.
"That can't be!" But he followed Duck as she looked in the water . . .

The moon was not there.
"Where has she gone?" cried Duck.

"The moon doesn't live in the pond!" laughed Squirrel, who was listening nearby. "She's above my nest in the fir tree."

"The moon doesn't live in a tree!" sniffed Duck.

"She does!" said Squirrel. He scampered around every branch, but he couldn't find the moon.

"She's not here!" he called down in a panic. "The wind must have blown her away!"

Rabbit was on his way home when he heard all the fuss.

"Blown the moon away?" he grinned. "Never! She was with me in the mountains."

"The moon doesn't go to the mountains!" said Squirrel.

"Of course she does!" stated Rabbit. They all dashed after him to find the moon.

Little Harvest Mouse searched the sky. Duck looked
in every pool and puddle. Squirrel scrambled in and out
of the trees, and Rabbit bounded high and low. But
they couldn't find the moon anywhere.
As the wind blew stronger, thunder
rumbled through the hills.

"What have you done with my moon, Squirrel?" snapped Duck.

"Rabbit must have lost her!" Squirrel whimpered.

"I've done no such thing!" grumbled Rabbit.

"But what will I do without her?" squeaked Mouse. "I'll be all alone!"

FLASH! BOOM! Lightning lit up the sky.

CRACK! CRASH! Thunder clattered over the mountains.

"Follow me!" shouted Rabbit. "I know where there's a cave!"

They
raced
through
the storm
and squeezed
together in
the cave.

"I'm sorry I snapped," whispered Duck.

"It was my fault," Squirrel piped up. "I shouldn't have blamed Rabbit."

"No harm done," said Rabbit bravely.

At last, the rain stopped and the clouds rumbled away.

"Look! Look!" cried Little Harvest Mouse.
The clear dark sky was full of twinkling stars,
and peeping out from among them was the moon!
It glowed bright over the mountains,
glittering through the trees and
shining in the pond . . .

"The same moon belongs to all of us," whispered Duck.

"She never really left us," said Squirrel.

"Good friends never do," nodded Rabbit wisely.

"And best of all," smiled Mouse, "she's given me three new friends!"